BALLARD SCHOOL

Birthday Book
Club

Donated in Honor of:

STAFF AND STUDENTS OF THE BALLARD

Donated on: _____ JUNE 13, 2003 _____

AUNT NINA'S VISIT

by Franz Brandenberg ❖ pictures by Aliki

GREENWILLOW BOOKS, NEW YORK

Library of Congress Cataloging in Publication Data

Brandenberg, Franz.
Aunt Nina's visit.
Summary: Aunt Nina's six kittens disrupt a
puppet show given by her nieces and nephews.
[1. Cats—Fiction.   2. Puppet plays—Fiction.
3. Plays—Fiction] I. Aliki, ill.   II. Title.
PZ7.B7364Aud 1984   [E]   83-16531
ISBN 0-688-01764-9
ISBN 0-688-01766-5 (lib. bdg.)

for
Pablo and Anna
Charles and Iona
Richard and Helena
their aunts and uncles
and especially
their grandmamá, M.W.

"There's nothing to do," said Alexandra.
"Go play with your friend," said her mother.
"She is away for the weekend," said Alexandra.
"How about your brother?" asked her father.
"It's boring to always play with your sister,"
 said Alex.
"I wish we had company!" said Alexandra.

The doorbell rang.
Alex and Alexandra ran to the door.
It was their cousins Bernard and Bernadette.
"My wish has come true," said Alexandra.

"Let's have a puppet show," said Alex.
"Bernard and I will work the puppets,
  Bernadette can work the lights,
  and Alexandra can play the piano."
"Who is going to be the audience?"
  asked Bernadette.
"It's no good performing for nobody,"
  said Bernard.

The doorbell rang.
All four children ran to the door.
It was their cousins Charles and Charlotte.

"We are going to have a puppet show," said Alex.
"Can I work the curtains?" asked Charlotte.
"Can I do the special effects?" asked Charles.
"We need you to be the audience," said Bernadette.
"That's not fair," said Charles and Charlotte.

The doorbell rang.
All six children ran to the door.
It was Aunt Nina.
"I brought you your kittens," she said.
"There is one for each of you."
"Thank you, Aunt Nina," said her nephews
and nieces. "It's just what we always wanted."

"They could be in our puppet show," said Alex.
"I don't think they'd like that," said Aunt Nina.
"They're not toys."
"Oh, look! They are running away,"
 said the nephews and nieces.
"Don't worry," said Aunt Nina.
"They'll be back when they are hungry.
"What about your puppet show?" she asked.
"We don't have an audience," said Bernard.
"I'll be the audience," said Aunt Nina.

They set up the puppet theater.
Bernadette switched on the footlights.
Charlotte opened the curtain.
"There they are!" said Aunt Nina.
The six little kittens were sitting on the stage.
"They like to be in our puppet show after all,"
said Alex.
"They like the warmth of the lights,"
said Aunt Nina.

Alexandra began to play the piano.
But the six little kittens stopped her.
Alex and Bernard tried to work the puppets.
But the six little kittens didn't let them.

Charles did a special effect.
That scared the six little kittens away.
Aunt Nina applauded.
"That was the funniest puppet show
I ever saw," she said.
"And you are the best audience we ever had,"
said the nephews and nieces.

"Lunch is ready!" said Mother.
They tried to sit at the table.
But the six little kittens didn't let them.

"Rest time," said Father.
They tried to rest.
But the six little kittens didn't let them.

It was time for the cousins to go.
Each chose a kitten to take home.
"I have to go too," said Aunt Nina.
"Come see me soon."
"We will," said the nephews and nieces.

"That was the best visit ever," said Alex.
"I wish we always had company," said Alexandra.
"Now we do," said Alex. "We have our kittens."